Milo opened the book to the first page, leaned against the wall, and began reading.

CHAPTER ONE

I Know What You're Thinking!

· · ·

You know what you're thinking? You're thinking, "How can a funny-looking guy like this Dr. K. Pinkerton Silverfish teach me how to become perfect?" Right?

Milo nodded.

Well, maybe I'm not as stupid as I look. After all, I guessed what you were thinking, didn't I?

You have just learned the first lesson in perfection. Things are not always what they seem.

You may turn the page.

Milo did.

Be a
Perfect Person
in Just
Three Days!

Be a Perfect Person in Just Three Days!

By STEPHEN MANES

Drawings by Tom Huffman

BANTAM BOOKS

NEW YORK • TORONTO • LONDON • SYDNEY • AUCKLAND

RL 6, 008-012

BE A PERFECT PERSON IN JUST THREE DAYS!

A Bantam Skylark Book / published by arrangement with Clarion Books

PRINTING HISTORY

Clarion Books edition published April 1982

Bantam edition / June 1983

Skylark Books is a registered trademark of Bantam Books, a division of Bantam Doubleday Dell Publishing Group, Inc. Registered in U.S. Patent and Trademark Office and elsewhere.

ISBN 0-553-15580-6

Published simultaneously in the United States and Canada

Bantam Books are published by Bantam Books, a division of Bantam Doubleday Dell Publishing Group, Inc. Its trademark, consisting of the words "Bantam Books" and the portrayal of a rooster, is Registered in U.S. Patent and Trademark Office and in other countries. Marca Registrada. Bantam Books, 1540 Broadway, New York, New York 10036.

PRINTED IN THE UNITED STATES OF AMERICA

OPM   30 29 28 27 26 25 24

for Esther

TALES OF SCARY MONSTERS
HORRIBLE
BOOK OF GORE
MORE FIENDS
BE A PERFECT PERSON IN JUST THREE DAYS
DEMONS
GHOULS
CREATURES
MONSTERS
MORE GORE
TERROR
WEREWOLVES

1

Some people want to be astronauts or ballet dancers or plumbers. Milo Crinkley wanted to be perfect.

It all began in the library. Milo was minding his own business, looking for a good scary monster story, when a book tumbled down from the top shelf and hit him on the head. First he felt his aching skull to make sure it was still in one piece. Then he picked up the book. The front cover screamed *Be a Perfect Person in Just Three Days!* It didn't look like any monster story Milo had ever read.

The author's picture was on the back. Dr. K. Pinkerton Silverfish did not look anything like Milo's idea of a doctor. He wore baggy zebra-striped pants that looked as though they might fall down any second, a shirt with palm trees on it and two buttons missing, one mitten, a clown nose, a bow tie with only half a bow, and a dented hat with a feather sticking up on each side. Dr. Silverfish was biting down on a hot dog, and mustard was dribbling down his chin. If you had to pick someone to teach you how to be perfect, Dr. Silverfish would not be high on your list.

Yet somehow—maybe getting hit on the head had scrambled his brains a little—Milo felt almost as though the book had jumped off the shelf, grabbed him, and hollered "Read me!" Besides, it was thin. It probably wouldn't take much time to finish.

Milo opened it to the first page, leaned against the wall, and began reading.

I Know What You're Thinking!

• • •

You know what you're thinking? You're thinking, "How can a funny-looking guy like this Dr. K. Pinkerton Silverfish teach me how to become perfect?" Right?

Milo nodded.

Well, maybe I'm not as stupid as I look. After all, I guessed what you were thinking, didn't I?

You have just learned the first lesson in perfection. Things are not always what they seem.

You may turn the page.

Milo did.

CHAPTER TWO

Who Says I Can Make You Perfect?

• • •

Who says I can make you perfect?
I do.
I, Dr. K. Pinkerton Silverfish, am an expert on perfection. If you don't believe it, just ask me.
Turn the page again. Isn't this easy?

Milo had never read an author quite like Dr. Silverfish. He turned the page.

CHAPTER THREE

You're Getting Better All the Time!

• • •

Very good. You turned the page. You can be trusted to follow orders. This is essential if you wish to become perfect.
Now I am going to tell you what you have to do if perfect is what you want to be. It will take you exactly three days. Each evening you will read exactly one

12

chapter of this book. You will follow my instructions precisely. At the end of the third day you will be perfect, and I will congratulate you.

BUT LET ME TELL YOU SOME-THING YOU'D BETTER NOT TRY.

Under no circumstances should you attempt to become perfect in less than three days. Whatever you do, don't read more than one chapter each day. Many people are tempted to sneak a look at the very last page before the third day is over. All I can say is, DON'T DO IT!

Suddenly Milo had a terrible urge to flip to the last page of the book and see what it had to say. It might save him a lot of unnecessary reading.

Dr. Silverfish glowered at him from the back cover, but Milo didn't care. He opened the back of the book, flipped past a couple of blank sheets, and found the last page with writing on it.

BOY, ARE YOU DUMB!

Didn't I tell you not to look at the last page of this book? Do you want to become perfect or don't you?

All right. I'll give you one more chance.

When you're finished with this page, shut the book. Some evening when you're ready to get serious about being perfect, open it to page ten. There you'll find instructions about what to do on day one of your program of perfection.

Now, shut the book, and don't say I didn't warn you.

Dr. Silverfish was definitely smarter than he looked. Milo shut the book,

He decided to take it home. Being perfect sounded pretty good to him. He was always getting into dumb accidents—knocking over his mother's expensive bud vase or sitting on his sister's brand-new record album or letting the bottom fall out of a bag of groceries (mostly eggs) on the way home from the

store. Or getting hit on the head by books in the library. Things like that obviously didn't happen to perfect people.

And he could just imagine what a welcome change it would be to hear people say, "Milo, you're perfect." His big sister Elissa wouldn't be able to tell him, "You sure are stupid, Milo," or "Don't be a pest, Milo," the way she did now. His parents would never have anything to bawl him out about. And perfection would probably come in handy in ways he hadn't thought of yet. Perfect was definitely a good thing to be, and Dr. Silverfish seemed to know all about it.

Milo checked out the book. Halfway home he remembered he'd forgotten about those monster stories he'd been looking for, but he didn't go back for them. After all, there was no telling what Dr. Silverfish might ask him to do. Becoming perfect might take up most of his time for the next three days.

2

Milo had two Creme-Stuft Twinkles and a glass of milk and went to his room to get his homework out of the way. It took him longer than usual, because his mind kept drifting to Dr. Silverfish's book.

Milo kept imagining what it would be like to be a perfect person. He'd be able to do anything he wanted to and do it right the first time. He would be able to throw out all his erasers. He could correct his teachers in front of the class and never be wrong. He'd get perfect scores on all his tests. Best of all,

nobody would ever have anything to scold him about. It sounded . . . well, perfect! He decided he'd read Dr. Silverfish's instructions right after dinner.

Of course, he was far from perfect yet. At dinner his father told him not to slurp his soup. His mother told him to quit eating so fast. And his sister told him to put his feet on his own side of the table.

Milo couldn't stand it. "I bet you'd love me if I turned perfect," he said.

His mother chuckled. "Not much chance of that, is there?"

"I'd settle for okay," said his father. "Nobody's perfect."

"Especially Milo," laughed Elissa.

"I'll show them," Milo thought. "Just three more days." And he gave his sister a kick under the table. There was no sense being perfect until he had to be.

After dinner Milo went upstairs, sat down at his desk, and picked up his copy of *Be a*

Perfect Person. Even with the clown nose, Milo decided, Dr. K. Pinkerton Silverfish looked extremely intelligent.

Milo began wondering what the K. stood for. Carefully, so he couldn't possibly stumble on anything he wasn't supposed to read yet, he opened the book to the inside back cover and found Dr. Silverfish's biography on the jacket flap.

> **Is Dr. K. Pinkerton Silverfish the world's leading authority on perfection? You bet your booties, Grandma!**
>
> **He is also Thompson Seedless Professor of Enology at the Ripple Campus of Skidrow College. He holds degrees from Fahrenheit University and Centigrade Institute, but when his arms get tired he puts them down. As a hobby, Dr. Silverfish raises Venus flytraps. He also owns the world's second largest collection of unusual toothpicks.**

Milo closed the book. His question remained unanswered, but he felt ready to begin. He took a very serious deep breath and opened the book to where he'd left off at the library.

**You Can't Take the Last Step
to Perfection Until You Take the First!**

• • •

I know what you're thinking again.

You're wondering what the K. in my name stands for.

Well, I'm not going to tell you. There are a lot more important things than wondering what the K. stands for, and that's why you're here. Close your eyes, count to ten, and open them again.

Milo did.

Wasn't that a lot more important than wondering what the K. stands for? Of course!

Now here are your instructions for the

21

first day. When you finish reading this, get a stalk of broccoli and tie a loop of string around the end. Leave it in your bedroom overnight. When you're all dressed tomorrow morning, put the string around your neck and wear the broccoli like a necklace. And don't take if off until I tell you to. See you tomorrow!

Milo couldn't believe his eyes. He turned the page.

Well, don't just sit there and stare! Go get the broccoli! And don't turn any more pages. Shut the book this instant!

Milo obeyed. He set the book down on his desk and looked at the picture of Dr. Silverfish. It was hard to tell because the doctor's hot dog blocked off his expression, but Milo thought the doctor might possibly be smirking at him.

Milo didn't think about it very long,

though. What he had to do now was find some broccoli.

He went down to the kitchen and opened the freezer. Underneath a bowl of Fake Whip, behind a bag of instant waffles, he found what he was looking for. "Broccoli," read the package, "in a delicious imitation cheese sauce made from only the finest, most succulent chemicals."

Dr. Silverfish hadn't said anything about imitation cheese sauce, but it was liable to be messy when it thawed out. Milo closed the freezer and opened the refrigerator. He was in luck. There in the crisper, right next to a plastic bag of carrots with a bucktoothed bunny on it, was a huge stalk of broccoli.

Milo wondered whether he should take it without mentioning it to somebody. Normally his parents didn't mind his taking things from the fridge, but usually what he took was milk or pie or pop or something. Vegetables were a different story. Milo couldn't remember taking a single vegetable out of the refrigerator, unless pickles and olives counted. He figured he'd better ask, just to be on the safe side.

Milo went into the living room, where his parents were watching the news. "Mom?"

"Hm?"

"Do you mind if I borrow some broccoli for a while?"

His mother shook her head. Milo wasn't sure if it meant she didn't mind or if she wanted him to be quiet so she could hear about the gorilla war at the zoo, but he decided it probably didn't matter much one way or the other. He took the broccoli upstairs, along with some string.

Milo had a hard time keeping his mind on anything but broccoli the rest of the evening. He wondered how in the world wearing a stalk of broccoli around his neck could possibly help make him perfect, and he was half-tempted to peek in Dr. Silverfish's book and try to find out. But he figured the doctor would probably outsmart him somehow, so he didn't bother. He'd been outsmarted once too often. Maybe that was part of the secret of being perfect, Milo thought: not letting people like Dr. Silverfish outsmart you. Well, he'd find out soon enough. Maybe.

That night Milo dreamed about being perfect. He was sitting on top of a huge piece of broccoli. A halo of green light surrounded him as he smiled down at all the imperfect people in the world and laughed at their mistakes. His sister bumped into the broccoli stalk and stubbed her toe, and Milo laughed and laughed. His mother locked her keys in the car, and Milo howled. His father dropped a big bag of groceries, and Milo roared. In fact, he laughed so hard he fell out of broccoli—or, rather, bed.

3

An almost perfect day, Milo thought as he looked out the window next morning. Milo himself, however, was a long way from perfection. As usual, he fought with his sister about who would use the bathroom first, and as usual, his sister won. Then Milo played his radio too loud, and his parents shouted for him to turn it down.

At last he was dressed. It was time to get serious. Milo stood in front of the mirror and picked up the broccoli. It looked rather tired and limp despite its night's rest. Milo put the string around his neck, and the broccoli dangled upside down in front of his chest. It was the dumbest-looking thing he'd ever seen, but he didn't dare laugh, because this was a matter of the utmost importance.

Then he realized he would have to eat breakfast and face his family with this green vegetable hanging from his neck. It was not going to be easy. He dawdled awhile.

"Milo!" called his mother from downstairs. "You're late for breakfast!"

Milo looked in the mirror and fiddled with the broccoli. He tried sticking it under his shirt, but all that did was make him lumpy. His family would never overlook a lump that size in a million years. Better to leave the broccoli out where everybody could admire it.

"Milo!" his father hollered. "Get down here!"

Milo went down the stairs and into the dining room. The minute his sister saw him, she laughed so hard she sprayed a mouthful of Oat Whammies all over the table. But his parents were too busy staring at Milo to scold her.

"What," his mother asked in astonishment, "is that?"

Milo tried to play dumb. "What do you mean?"

"That thing hanging from your neck," said his father.

"Oh, that," said Milo calmly. "That's a stalk of broccoli."

"Sure, Dad," said Elissa. "Lots of people walk around with stalks of broccoli hanging from their necks. That's how you can tell the morons from the rest of us."

Milo made a face at her. She made a worse one back.

"Would you mind telling me just what you think you're doing?" his mother inquired.

"I'm wearing this broccoli around my neck."

"Is this some kind of new fad or something?" asked his father.

"No," said Milo, trying hard to think of an explanation that would satisfy his parents. "We're . . . uh . . . doing a play in school about nutrition. I'm one of the vegetables."

"Good thing you're not the watermelon," said his sister. "You wouldn't be able to stand up straight."

"Do you have to wear this broccoli at the breakfast table?" Mrs. Crinkley asked.

"Yes," Milo replied. "It helps me remember my lines."

His mother gave a deep sigh. "Milo, that broccoli is for tonight's dinner. Be sure to put it back in the fridge when you get home from school."

"I can't," said Milo, feeling sillier by the minute.

"Why not?"

Milo thought very hard. "Because I need to wear it tonight, too."

"I thought you said the play was today."

"No. Today's only a rehearsal. The play is really tomorrow."

"If you ask me, I've got a broccoli-brain for a brother," said Elissa.

"All right, Milo," Mrs. Crinkley sighed. "By the time it finishes walking around with you all day, that broccoli won't be fit for human consumption anyhow. We'll use up the leftover rutabaga tonight."

"Not rutabaga again!" cried Elissa, sticking her tongue out in disgust. For once Milo tended to agree with her.

Well, nobody said being perfect was going to be easy, thought Milo as he stepped out the front door. It was a beautiful spring day, much too warm to even think about wearing a jacket. There was no way to hide his broccoli, and of course it was the first thing everybody noticed on the way to school.

"What's *that* for?" asked Milo's classmate George, making a face and pointing.

"I've got a terrible disease," said Milo. "The

32

only cure for it is to wear broccoli around your neck for a whole day. Then you throw the broccoli away and the disease is gone."

"What's this disease called?" George asked suspiciously.

"It's a long name," said Milo. "I can't remember."

"You're lying, Milo," said Janet. "I've never heard of any disease like that."

"Me, neither." George stepped in front of Milo and blocked his path. "Give me that!" he ordered, and grabbed for the broccoli, but Milo jumped aside.

Usually Milo backed down when George bullied him, but this time he was totally unafraid. George grabbed again, but Milo kept leaping away, holding on to the broccoli for dear life. Finally George got tired and gave up. He wasn't used to Milo's defending himself.

"Milo, that broccoli is the stupidest thing I've ever seen," Janet declared.

"Why?" Milo asked. "People wear all sorts

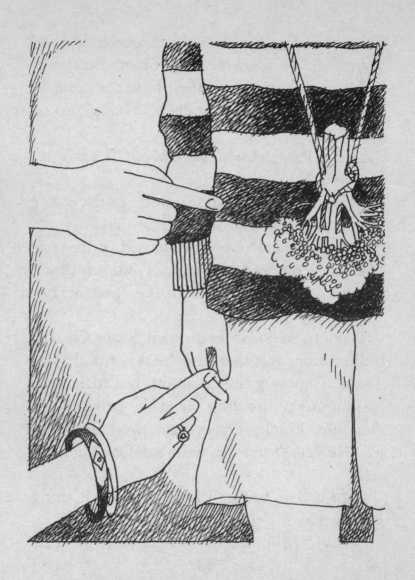

of things around their necks. Why not broccoli?"

"Why not cauliflower?" George scoffed, making another futile grab at Milo's vegetable. "Why not a ham and cheese sandwich? Because it's stupid, that's why."

"Look, nobody's making you wear anything," Milo shot back. "If I have to wear this, it's my business. If you don't like it, leave me alone."

George backed off, shaking his head. "Well, at least I don't have to eat it. If there's one vegetable I hate, it's broccoli."

The rest of Milo's day was rather embarrassing. He was the center of attention in every class. When his teachers asked him why he was wearing a stalk of broccoli around his neck, he told them it was his doctor's orders, and yes, he had a horrible disease, and no, he didn't know what it was called, but it wasn't supposed to be contagious. The hardest part was gym, because the broccoli kept flopping around while he did his exercises. The only other real problem was that the vegetable began to develop a rather pungent odor and started dropping little green flowers all over his shirt.

Milo felt very proud of himself the rest of the day. At dinner he tried to be as perfect as he could, now that he was in training. He ignored his sister's snide remarks about broccoli-wearers, he politely asked people to pass the dishes instead of reaching for them himself, and he even said thank you when he got them.

"Thank you!" echoed his mother. "You know, Milo, I'm beginning to think that broccoli is having a strange effect on your brain! If it's going to make you behave like this, I think I'll *make* you wear it."

Milo didn't say anything. He just smiled the most perfect smile he could and cut his rutabaga into tiny bite-sized pieces so that he could chew and digest it with absolute perfection.

4

After dinner, Milo rushed upstairs and picked up Dr. Silverfish's book. He was so excited he was almost afraid to open it, but the doctor seemed to be staring back at him with a look that said "Quit staring at me and open the book," so Milo did.

DAY TWO

Think of It!
You're Getting Closer All the Time!

• • •

But what are you doing sitting there with a stalk of broccoli around your

neck? Why, that's the stupidest thing I've ever seen! Don't even think about turning the page until you take it off.

Milo was surprised at Dr. Silverfish's reaction, but he removed the broccoli gladly. Then he turned the page:

Well, that's more like it. Imagine, coming to a famous doctor like me with a stalk of broccoli dangling in front of you! All I can say is, you must have a lot of courage. In fact, you must be absolutely fearless. It is a well-known fact that there is nothing in the entire world more humiliating than wearing a stalk of broccoli around your neck.

So just think: you have nothing more to fear for the rest of your life. Even if you put your pants on backwards or wear two different-colored socks, a hat with grapes on it, and a diaper, you will never look as stupid as you did a moment ago. Obviously you will never be embarrassed again.

Congratulations! You have conquered fear, and that's the first step toward being perfect.

Now for step two. From now until exactly this time tomorrow, don't eat. What do I mean? I mean, don't eat. Or drink, except for water. No food or drink, period. No liver, no octopus, no chocolate-covered shrimp, no pistachio ice cream sodas with whipped chili topping—not even boring foods like pepperoni-and-pineapple pizza. Nothing!

Cheat on this one, and you'll never be perfect. So . . . until tomorrow . . . stay hungry!

Milo looked at his watch. It read six-fifty-two. How could he not eat until six-fifty-two the next day? It was impossible. If only he'd known, he would've stoked up with extra-big helpings at dinner, but now he couldn't even have his bedtime snack. It hadn't been more than a few minutes since dessert, but Milo already felt hungry. And miserable. Here he was starving, yet if he wanted to become perfect, there was no way he could eat anything. Not even broccoli.

Still, he was determined not to give up. After tossing the broccoli in the wastebasket, he decided he'd try to take his mind off his stomach. He went downstairs to the living room to watch TV.

"Hey, where's your broccoli?" his sister demanded.

Milo thought fast. "Oh, I already know all my lines by heart."

"Yeah? Let's hear!"

Milo improvised. "I am a broccoli, big and green . . ."

"That's plenty," Elissa interrupted, and turned back to her program.

Milo tried to watch it too, but the ads for hamburgers and fish sandwiches and soft drinks and candies only made him hungrier. He went to his room and turned on the radio, but that was no better. He tried reading a book, but it began with a family at the dinner table, and he just couldn't stomach it.

Finally he lay down and went to sleep. All night long he dreamed of pies and cakes and pork chops that looked absolutely perfect. But he couldn't eat them, even in his dream.

It was very frustrating. At least he didn't dream about broccoli. He'd had quite enough of broccoli for a while.

In the morning he awoke with the biggest appetite of his life. He didn't fight with his sister over who'd use the bathroom first, since he didn't think perfect people did things like that, and he was too weak to argue anyhow. It seemed to take him forever to get dressed.

"Milo!" his father shouted. "Come downstairs to breakfast!"

"I'm not going to eat breakfast today," Milo yelled back feebly.

"What's wrong? Are you sick?"

"No. I just don't want anything to eat."

"You come downstairs, and we'll discuss it!"

Milo didn't even want to look at food, because he was so hungry he might break down and eat something and miss out on becoming perfect. But he went downstairs anyhow.

His mother was spreading a big spoonful of strawberry jam on a piece of raisin toast. "What's this about your not wanting breakfast?" she asked.

"I'm not going to eat anything this morning," Milo said reluctantly.

"Milo had too much broccoli yesterday," laughed Elissa, shoving half an instant waffle into her mouth.

"Milo, something doesn't seem quite right with you," said his father between gulps of tomato juice. "First the broccoli, and now this. Do you feel all right?"

Milo nodded weakly.

"Are you sure?" asked his father.

Milo tried to act peppier. "I'm fine," he said.

"Won't you at least have some juice?"

"No. I'm just not hungry."

"Suit yourself," said his father. "Missing one meal never hurt anybody."

Milo looked longingly at the cereal, the

milk, the juice, the toast, the jelly, the butter,
and the instant waffles. He tried not to inhale
too deeply, but aromas kept reaching out and
tickling his nose. So he felt very proud that
he was able to resist temptation and make it

to school without having anything but three large glasses of water.

His classmates kept asking him where his broccoli was today, but Milo told them his illness was cured. The kids called him things like "Broccolihead" and "The Human Vegetable," but now that he knew he was fearless, those names didn't bother him. Besides, he felt sort of like a human vegetable.

By the time lunch hour rolled around, Milo was positively starving, but he was more determined than ever not to eat. He offered his peanut butter and alfalfa sprout sandwich to anybody who wanted it, but he had to feed it to the pigeons. Nobody else was willing to risk catching Milo's strange disease. At the water fountain, Milo held up the line until everybody yelled "Save some for the fishes!" in chorus for the fifth time.

Milo had a lot of trouble getting through the afternoon. His stomach started to complain, and it simply refused to shut up. In the middle of Miss Lextor's English class, it made embarrassing gurgles. During music class, it kept singing off-key. The teachers were kind enough to ignore it, but the kids never stopped giggling. All Milo could do was give them a look as if to say, "I told you I was sick!" and send silent messages to his stomach to quiet down.

After school Milo trudged home. His sister was having an afternoon snack of carrot cake and milk. Just looking at the food made Milo feel weak. He went straight upstairs to lie down.

Next thing he knew, his sister was yelling at him to come down to dinner. Still half asleep, he groggily told her he'd be right there. Then he remembered he couldn't eat anything for another hour or so. Suddenly the smell of his favorite food—sweet-and-sour won ton from Bo Wo's To Go Restaurant in the shopping center—wafted up to him from the dining room.

"Dinnertime, Milo!" yelled his father. "Your food's getting cold!"

The wonton smelled wonderful. Milo had to make a superhuman effort to resist. "I'm not hungry!" he said weakly.

A minute later, Mr. Crinkley came upstairs and stormed into Milo's room. "What's all this foolishness?" he demanded. "Are you feeling sick?"

"Yes," said Milo, and it wasn't a lie.

"How?"

"My stomach has kind of an empty feeling."

"Why don't you come downstairs and fill it up?"

"I don't feel like it," Milo said. "Maybe I have the flu. Maybe I'll be able to eat something later."

Just then a book on Milo's desk caught Mr. Crinkley's eye. It was a thin volume and it had a picture of a peculiar-looking man on the back. Milo hoped his dad wouldn't start flipping through it, but that's exactly what he did.

"*Be a Perfect Person in Just Three Days!*" his father said. "Have you been reading this?"

Milo didn't quite know what to say. Even though he knew he was fearless, he felt slightly embarrassed. "Well, sort of . . ."

Mr. Crinkley looked at the book some more. "It says here you're not supposed to eat anything on Day Two. Is that what you're up to?"

Milo nodded weakly.

"So that explains it!" His father laughed. "Why didn't you tell us?"

"I thought everybody would laugh at me, and that's just what you're doing," Milo moaned. "Besides, I wanted to be perfect and surprise you."

"I'm not laughing at you," said Mr. Crinkley, and buried his nose in the book again. He was a very fast reader. Milo watched him raise his eyebrows and wrinkle his nose and scratch his ear as he scanned the pages. Then Mr. Crinkley shut the book and laid it back on the desk. "You know, Milo, it might be nice to have one perfect person in the family."

"Please don't tell Mom about it. Or especially Elissa. It's hard enough already, without her making funny remarks."

"My lips are sealed," said Mr. Crinkley. "How much longer till you're perfect?"

"Tomorrow night, I hope."

"Well, good luck. I'm going down to dinner." And Milo's father went out the door.

Milo lay on his bed and listened to his stomach growl until about six-thirty. He had read Dr. Silverfish's last commands at exactly six-fifty-two last night, so he had to wait until six-fifty-three tonight (since his watch always ran a little fast) to see what Dr. Silverfish wanted him to do next. Milo never knew time could creep by so slowly. A minute seemed like an hour. Five minutes might as well have been a year. Maybe when you were almost perfect, time went slower.

The hands of his watch crept forward. Six-fifty. Six-fifty-one. Six-fifty-two. Six fifty-two and a half. Six fifty-two and three-quarters. Six-fifty- . . . three! Milo grabbed the book and pawed it open.

I'll Bet You Could Eat a Horse!

• • •

Hungry? Naturally!
Please don't eat a horse. Anything else
is okay. When you're finished eating,
turn the page.

Milo stuck a baseball card in the book to
mark his place and went downstairs. The rest
of the family was watching TV. "I think I
could eat something now," Milo said.

"Too late," Elissa sneered. "We finished
every last won ton."

"Feeling better?" his mother asked.

"Yes," said Milo. "Hungry, even."

"I can rustle something up for you if you
can wait until this program's over," said his
father.

Milo couldn't wait. "Don't bother," he said.
He went into the kitchen and fixed himself an

excellent supper. He had a sardine sandwich, a peanut butter sandwich, and a bologna sandwich, an apple, an orange, a pear, and a banana, four pieces of butter crumb cake, three oatmeal raisin cookies, and two huge helpings of cherry vanilla ice cream with chocolate fudge sauce. Plus a piece of strawberry-rhubarb pie for dessert. It wasn't sweet-and-sour won ton, but it all tasted terrific. Afterwards Milo felt a lot better, even though his stomach sent up a few strange-flavored burps of protest.

5

When Milo went back upstairs and picked up the book, he thought Dr. Silverfish looked extremely sly. It was almost as though he was going to say something he knew Milo wouldn't want to hear. Milo opened the book and began reading.

DAY THREE

Take the Last Step to Perfection!

• • •

I'll bet that tasted good.

And to top it off, you're more nearly perfect than ever. Perfect people do not eat very often. Eating gives you too many chances to dribble ketchup down your chin.

Now, it is a well-known fact that there is nothing more difficult than going without food for an entire day. But you did it. This proves you can do something just because you want to, which is what we experts call "will power."

Some inferior minds call it "stick-to-it-iveness." Not me. But you have proven that even if you think something's nearly impossible, like learning Finnish or becoming a classical kazoo player or building a model of the Eiffel Tower out of chewing gum, you'll be able to stick to it and get it done if you really want to. This is a very important lesson on the road to perfection.

After today's lesson, your final assignment should be a snap. Ready?

Milo remembered Dr. Silverfish's sly look. He had the feeling something unpleasant was coming. He read on:

Right now, you are thinking that I am going to ask you to do something horribly difficult, something you have never done before, something you won't possibly be able to do even if you try your hardest.

Well, you're wrong. All I want you to do is go to the nearest zoo and bring home a fully-grown gorilla.

Milo's jaw dropped. He couldn't believe it. He turned the page.

Just kidding! We doctors enjoy our little jokes once in a while. If you went out and brought home a gorilla because you didn't keep on reading, I apologize. To the gorilla. He's stuck with a dummy like you. You get no apology, because you were stupid. What do gorillas have to do with being perfect, anyhow? Broccoli is another story.

Now you are wondering if I will ever get to the point and tell you what to do on your last day of my perfection course. Well, the answer is no. I won't tell you to do anything, because what I want you to do is nothing. That's pretty simple, isn't it? Don't eat, don't sleep, don't watch TV, don't listen to music, don't read, don't crochet, don't play cards, don't snap your fingers, don't pick your nose, don't even whistle. Don't do a single thing for the next twenty-four hours. Sit! Think. Relax. Be like broccoli.

See you tomorrow. By then you'll be perfect.

P. S. I realize it is hard to start doing nothing all at once. You may warm up by practicing doing nothing for ten minutes. The twenty-four hours will begin right after that.

P. P. S. It is okay to go to the bathroom. And sip weak tea slowly. And breathe. Everything else is a no-no.

Well, it sounded dumb, but it sounded simple enough. The hardest part would be not eating, but Milo knew he'd be able to handle that. The only problem was that tomorrow was Saturday, the day of Milo's weekly baseball game. He always played right field because he wasn't very good at baseball, but he liked it anyway.

Mostly what he did in right field was stand around. For a minute he wondered if Dr. Silverfish would consider playing right field to be doing nothing since it usually came pretty close. But Milo realized if a ball came near him he'd either have to let it go by or ruin all his plans for perfection. It would also be pretty silly to go up to the plate and not even take a swing. And just going up to bat was doing something, really. He decided he would just have to skip baseball this week.

Suddenly Milo noticed he was absent-mindedly tapping his fingers on his desk. He stopped in mid-tap. He'd have to watch that sort of thing. Tapping your fingers was doing something, even if it wasn't doing much. Luckily the warm-up period wasn't over yet.

Milo began thinking about the best way to do nothing. Then his father came in. Mr. Crinkley handed Milo a plastic cup and a big glass jar full of a brown fluid. "What's this?" Milo asked.

"Weak tea," said Mr. Crinkley. "Thought you might need it."

"You're only supposed to read this book a little at a time," Milo scolded. "You must've read the whole thing at once before dinner."

"Pretty near," his father admitted. "Never said *I* was perfect. Anyhow, I made a 'Do Not Disturb' sign for your door. I'll tell Mom and Elissa you're not to be bothered. See you tomorrow night. Good luck."

"Thanks, Dad."

Milo's father left the room. Milo opened the tea jar, took a sniff, made a face, and set the jar on the floor. Now there was nothing to do but think, relax, and vegetate. The idea of not sleeping was the part Milo liked best. He would have to stay up all night, something he had never done before. It would probably be more fun if he could listen to the radio, but Dr. Silverfish had specifically vetoed that.

Milo started thinking about how wonderful it would be to be perfect. He wouldn't have to bother going to school anymore. What could anybody teach a perfect person? Maybe he could become a major leaguer, the world's best pitcher. He'd throw only perfect games.

He was so close now. If only he could hang on for one more day, he would be the only perfect person he had ever met. But after about half an hour, he couldn't think of much more to think about. When it came to perfection he was all thought out.

He tried thinking about Dr. Silverfish, but he'd already thought about him about as much as he wanted to. He listened to the sounds of the traffic on the street. It was sort of interesting trying to sort out the cars from the motorcycles and trucks for a while, but then the traffic noises died down and got boring. He listened to his stomach digest his dinner, but after churning and gurgling for a few minutes, it developed laryngitis and hushed to a whisper. A few sips of tea helped his stomach regain its voice, but it tended to repeat itself the second time around.

There had to be other things to do, Milo thought, but then he remembered that doing things was exactly what he wasn't supposed to be doing. He tried to pick out pictures in the shadows on his wall, but the only one he could find looked like his grumpy math teacher.

He tried listening again. The TV was on downstairs, but he couldn't hear it clearly, and he thought he might be cheating if he could. Somebody was going to the bathroom down the hall. Milo glanced at his watch: it was only ten. He had a whole night of nothing to look forward to, followed by a very long and nothing day.

He tried to think of something else to think

of, but it was no use. He stared at his watch. It seemed to be running even slower than it had when he was waiting for dinner. He began to get drowsy. He wished he could read or play solitaire or build a model plane or something. He began to wonder if he'd ever be perfect after all.

Then he remembered a book he'd read about an old Indian custom. To become a man, a boy went into the forest naked on the coldest night of the year and had to come back the next morning with an eagle feather. Or maybe it was a condor feather. Something like that. Milo decided that if people could do those things, he could certainly do nothing long enough to become perfect.

Milo heard his sister go to bed, and then his parents. He realized he was probably the only one awake in the whole house. At three minutes after midnight he heard an airplane go by way off in the distance. At eighteen minutes to one, a car horn tooted outside and

a dog barked back. Then it was absolutely silent and still.

At two-something—he wasn't quite sure when—Milo's eyelids fell shut. He snapped them open again just as he was about to fall asleep. But as the nightlike early morning wore on, those eyelids kept getting heavier and heavier. Milo thought about standing up and jumping around, but he didn't, because that would be doing something. Eventually he got up and went to the bathroom, mostly to keep himself awake.

He came back and sat down again. A moment later, he saw his room fill up with light so white and brilliant he could hardly bear to look at it. As his eyes adjusted, he began to see people sitting in front of him. It was like being in an enormous auditorium with seats stretching as far as he could see. The people in the seats didn't move a muscle. They didn't make a sound. They were doing absolutely nothing—just like Milo.

From where he sat, all Milo could see were the backs of heads. He wanted to get up and walk around to find out what the people looked like. But he knew that would be doing something. He stayed put.

Then he realized people were sitting behind and beside him. To look at them, he only had to turn his head. But his head wouldn't move. He couldn't even shift his eyes. That would be doing something.

Then he noticed the person in front of him raise a glass to his lips. Milo would've had to lean forward to see the person's face, but he didn't have to do anything at all to see what was in the glass. It looked exactly like weak tea.

It was as though a sign had dropped in front of Milo's nose. "These must be perfect people," he said to himself. "Maybe I'm one of them already. Maybe time went by so fast I didn't notice."

Milo took a sip of his own tea and tried to

be as perfect as he knew how. Since he wasn't
able to move, except to sip his tea, all he
could do was watch the back of the neck of

the person in front of him. It was not a very exciting neck.

Milo grew fidgety. His nose began to itch. But he found he couldn't scratch it. He couldn't twiddle his thumbs, either, or tap out a rhythm on his chair. Perfect people obviously didn't do that sort of thing.

As the minutes dragged by, Milo began wondering what they *did* do. The answer seemed to be "Nothing." Milo had never been so bored in his entire life. He felt as though years were going by. He began to wonder if perfection was all it was cracked up to be.

Suddenly the light grew dim. Milo felt himself falling. He tumbled from his chair.

The perfect people all disappeared. The bedroom returned to normal. His watch showed nine-thirty. It was light out.

Milo felt sick. He had not made it to perfection after all. He had only fallen asleep. He had failed.

6

Milo was shattered. All that work, and now he'd never be perfect. At first he thought he would start over with Day One and the broccoli, but he decided it would be useless. And there was no sense trying to pretend he'd never fallen asleep. Dr. Silverfish would realize exactly what he was up to.

Milo picked up the book. Dr. Silverfish looked at him with a knowing smile. Milo did not smile back. He just opened the book.

**CONGRATULATIONS!
YOU'RE PERFECT!**
What more is there to say?
Unless by some strange chance you
did not follow my instructions precisely.
In which case, turn the page.

Milo felt awful. But he turned the page anyway.

**CONGRATULATIONS!
YOU'RE NOT PERFECT!**
It's ridiculous to want to be perfect anyway. But then, everybody's ridiculous sometimes, except perfect people.
You know what perfect is? Perfect is not eating or drinking or talking or moving a muscle or making even the teensiest mistake. Perfect is never doing anything wrong—which means never doing anything at all. Perfect is boring!

Suddenly Milo remembered that auditorium full of perfect people. He brightened a little as he turned the page.

So you're not perfect! Wonderful! Have fun! Eat things that give you bad breath! Trip over your own shoelaces! Laugh! Let somebody else laugh at you!

Perfect people never do any of those things. All they do is sit around and sip weak tea and think about how perfect they are. But they're not really one-hundred-percent perfect anyway. You should see them when they get the hiccups!

Milo smiled. He could just imagine a whole auditorium full of perfect hiccupers.

Phooey! Who needs 'em?

You can drink pickle juice and imitate gorillas and do silly dances and sing stupid songs and wear funny hats and be as imperfect as you please and still be a good person. Good people are hard to find nowadays. And they're a lot more fun than perfect people any day of the week.

Milo was feeling a lot better. He turned the page.

> Well, this is the last page. So in conclusion, I say to you:
> Thanks for tuning in.
> That's all till next time.
> Be good.
> If you still want to be perfect, go back to page one and start over. You are obviously a slow learner.
> And now I must be going. One of my Venus flytraps seems to be attacking my most unusual toothpick.
> Good-bye!
> P. S. Be sure to watch for my new book, *Make Four Billion Dollars by Next Thursday!*

Milo closed the book. It was hard to tell, but Dr. Silverfish almost seemed to be winking at him from the back cover.

Milo went downstairs. His dad was in the living room reading the paper. "Milo!" he exclaimed. "What are you doing down here?"

"I fell asleep," Milo said. "I just woke up."

"You mean to say you won't be perfect after all?"

Milo grinned. "I guess not."

"Maybe it's just as well," said his father. "I don't know if I could stand living with a perfect person."

"What do you mean?" Elissa said, coming down the stairs. "*I'm* perfect."

"You sure are," Milo replied. "Perfectly obnoxious. And we can't stand living with you!"

Ducking the roller skate Elissa threw at him, Milo laughed and went into the kitchen. He fixed himself a breakfast of pickles and salami. He whistled a stupid tune he'd made up. He made a horrible face at himself in the living-room mirror. He felt human again.

Milo found his mom and·got her to drive him to the baseball field just in time for the game. Any other day he would have wished he hadn't. He dropped a fly ball for a triple, he let a grounder skip through his legs for a

home run, and he struck out with the bases
loaded. His teammates got angry with him,
and even the manager looked annoyed.

Normally Milo would have been upset
with himself. But today he was calm.

"Nobody's perfect," he said with a shrug. And then he went out and made a brilliant catch of a long fly ball. It wasn't enough to save the game for his team, but it felt good. If you never dropped a ball or struck out, baseball would be as boring as sipping weak tea.

That afternoon, Milo took Dr. Silverfish's book back to the library. He was through with perfection for good.

A few weeks later, one of his classmates came to school with a stalk of broccoli dangling from her neck. A perfect person might have given her a few words of helpful advice.

Not Milo. He just took a bite of his garlic-and-stinky-cheese sandwich and wiped up the mustard that dribbled down his chin. He didn't say a word.

About the Author

STEPHEN MANES is a native of Pittsburgh, the world's most nearly perfect city. He has written perfectly good scripts for movies and television and perfectly hilarious columns for *PC/Computing* magazine. He is perfectly delighted that children in five states have voted this book their favorite of the year.

Mr. Manes is the author of *Make Four Million Dollars by Next Thursday!*, the sequel to this book, in which Dr. K. Pinkerton Silverfish makes his perfectly triumphant return. Mr. Manes has also created many other perfectly wonderful books, including *Chicken Trek, It's New! It's Improved! It's Terrible!, The Great Gerbil Roundup, Monstra vs. Irving, Chocolate-Covered Ants,* and *The Obnoxious Jerks.*

Mr. Manes lives in a perfect house in the perfectly charming community of Seattle, Washington. How does he describe his life as a writer? "It's okay, I guess."

About the Artist

TOM HUFFMAN was raised in Lexington, Kentucky, and received a fine arts degree from the University of Kentucky. He has created not only fine art and illustration, but jewelry, graphic design, fabrics, posters, and greeting cards. He has previously illustrated two books of plays by Sue Alexander, *Whatever Happened to Uncle Albert?* and *Small Plays for Special Days.*